April Hughes lives amongst the trees of the beautiful Pacific Northwest with her husband, two dogs, and a very boisterous parrot.

April discovered the joy of reading at a very early age, thus finding that friends and incredible adventures all over the world were as close as the tips of her fingers when turning the pages of a book. After a varied and interesting career-life, she decided to turn her love of reading into creating even more friends to be found by children of all ages. This is her first children's book.

"NO!"

April C. Hughes

AUSTIN MACAULEY PUBLISHERS™

LONDON • CAMBRIDGE • NEW YORK • SHARJAH

Copyright © April C. Hughes (2020)

Ordering Information:
Quantity sales: special discounts are available on quantity purchases by corporations, associations, and others. For details, contact the publisher at the address below.

Publisher's Cataloging-in-Publication data
Hughes, April C.
"NO!"

ISBN 9781643789736 (Paperback)
ISBN 9781643789743 (Hardback)
ISBN 9781645365792 (ePub e-book)

Library of Congress Control Number: 2019914087

www.austinmacauley.com/us

First Published (2020)
Austin Macauley Publishers LLC
40 Wall Street, 28th Floor
New York, NY 10005
USA
mail-usa@austinmacauley.com
+1 (646) 5125767

This book is dedicated to Donna Matthews, my friend, who inspired this adventure from beginning to end.

Many thanks to Margaret Nathon, for her insight; Timothy Bollenbaugh, for his artistic eye; Richard Hughes, for his unwavering encouragement; and to Judy Doyle, for just being Judy.

I would be totally remiss if I did not thank the production staff of Austin Macauley Publishers for patiently guiding this novice on this fascinating journey.

There once was a boy who would only say "No",
he would not say stop, he would not say go.

He would not say red, he would not say blue.
When going to bed there was no, "I love you."

His parents fretted then consumed with concern,
they took him to doctors, the cause to discern.

The doctors knocked on his knees and looked down his throat,
They poked and they prodded 'til the boy almost broke.

They conferred, then declared, "You've only to wait.
He'll outgrow this problem by the time he is eight."

His parents waited while trying their best,
did everything possible to coax just one yes.

They offered him cookies, they offered him cake
and a Disney vacation they all would take.

8

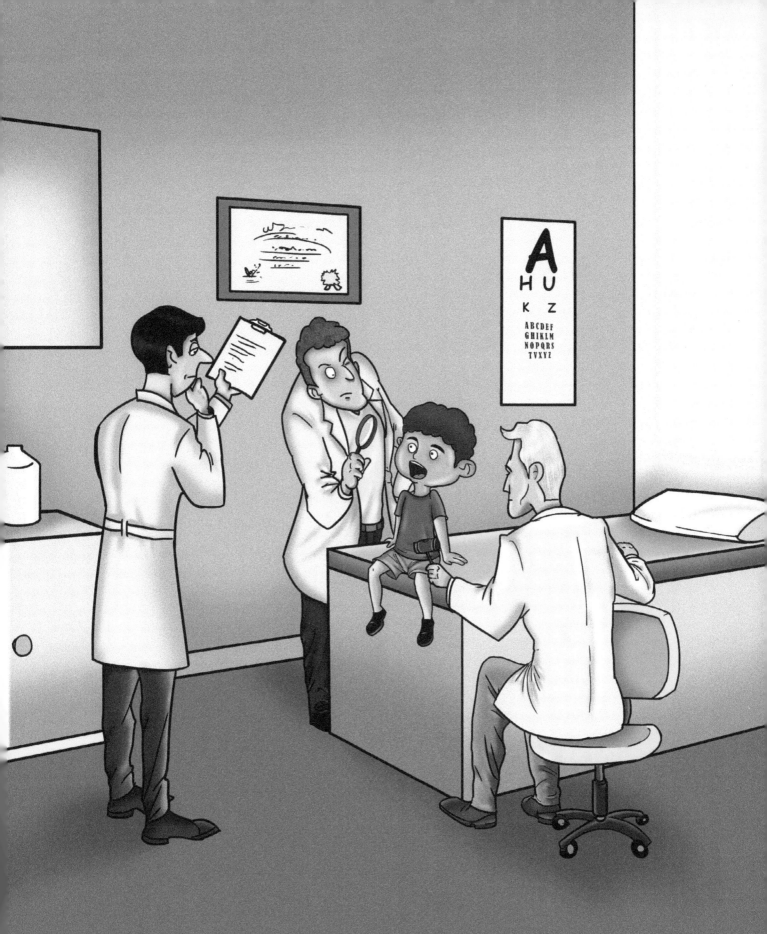

The boy raised his head and slouched down low
then at the top of his lungs bellowed, "NO, NO, NO, NO."

As time marched on, the parents filled with despair,
the boy had no friends-he did not even care.

Special tutors were engaged from the first school day,
even they could not change what the boy would not say.

Then a new student one day would appear,
she was sunny and lively, all full of good cheer.

They seemed to be opposites, as opposite could be.
They seemed to be as opposite as a bird and a tree.

The boys skin was caramel, the girls was like cream,
his hair was all curly–hers smooth as a jelly bean.

Her mouth showed all smiles where his only frowned,
he sat all alone, she had friends all around.

Though seemingly different, they felt a connect,
she hid a problem most wouldn't suspect.

When asked if she wanted a dress of bright blue,
she would say "yes," knowing that was not true.

She frolicked with kittens when frogs she preferred,
she loved to play soccer, but dolls she endured.

The source of her problem, you might now guess,
this cheery, bright girl could only say, "Yes."

One day after school on the way home,
the boy had decided to go for a roam.

16

He spied the girl at the edge of the park,
talking to a man where the shade turned to dark.

"You look a kind girl with a very big heart,
help me find my dog and I will give you a tart."

The man took her arm and led her away,
"Yes, yes," were the words the boy heard her say.

Though the boy had heard yes, it could not be true.
He needed to decide just what he should do.

Something changed in the boy at that moment in time,
his whole world shifted and turned on a dime.

The boy started running, shouting, "NO! NO! NO! NO!"
His legs moving faster than he thought they could go.

The man was quite startled, he gasped in alarm,
the girl gave a jerk, and he then freed her arm.

24

She fled to the boy, he grabbed her hand,
they ran and they ran until neither could stand.

Thus began a friendship never to end,
a bond not to break, not even to bend.

She taught the boy "Yes" and he taught her "No,"
a gift for both that continues to grow.

They hope their story shows with a friend by your side,
your journey through life is a far better ride!

CPSIA information can be obtained
at www.ICGtesting.com
Printed in the USA
LVHW071536011120
670397LV00015B/1420